AQUARIUS

AQUARIUS

AQUARIUS

AQUARIUS

每個人心中都有一座島嶼，
藉文字呼息而靜謐，
Island，我們心靈的岸。

露伊絲・葛綠珂（Louise Glück）著　陳育虹 譯

The Wild Iris

野鳶尾

《野鳶尾》

目錄

目錄

《野鳶尾》

FOR   獻給
Kathryn Davis   凱絲琳・戴維思
Meredith Hoppin   梅瑞迪・霍蘋
David Langston   大衛・藍斯頓

FOR   獻給
John and Noah   約翰與諾亞

The Wild Iris

At the end of my suffering
there was a door.

Hear me out: that which you call death
I remember.

Overhead, noises, branches of the pine shifting.
Then nothing. The weak sun
flickered over the dry surface.

It is terrible to survive
as consciousness
buried in the dark earth.

Then it was over: that which you fear, being
a soul and unable
to speak, ending abruptly, the stiff earth
bending a little. And what I took to be
birds darting in low shrubs.

野鳶尾

我痛苦的盡頭
有一扇門

你聽我說：你名之為死的
我記得

頭頂上有噪音，松枝搖曳
一切歸零。衰弱的太陽
在乾燥地表閃動

活著
很恐怖，當意識
埋入黑暗地底

一切就過去了——你的
畏懼：擔心化為幽靈
無法說話，草草結束了，僵硬的
泥土稍微凹陷；以及亂竄在灌木叢
我誤以為是飛鳥的，甚麼

You who do not remember
passage from the other world
I tell you I could speak again: whatever
returns from oblivion returns
to find a voice:

from the center of my life came
a great fountain, deep blue
shadows on azure seawater.

不記得曾經穿越過另‧世界的
你啊，讓我告訴你
我又能說話了；一切自湮沒
回來的，回來
為尋找發聲

自我生命中央噴出
一柱泉湧，鬱鬱的深藍
投影在碧藍海藍

Matins

The sun shines; by the mailbox, leaves
of the divided birch tree folded, pleated like fins.
Underneath, hollow stems of the white daffodils,
    Ice Wings, Cantatrice; dark
leaves of the wild violet. Noah says
depressives hate the spring, imbalance
between the inner and the outer world. I make
another case—being depressed, yes, but in a sense passionately
attached to the living tree, my body
actually curled in the split trunk, almost at peace,
    in the evening rain
almost able to feel
sap frothing and rising: Noah says this is
an error of depressives, identifying
with a tree, whereas the happy heart
wanders the garden like a falling leaf, a figure for
the part, not the whole.

晨禱

陽光耀眼；信箱旁分岔的

白樺樹葉合攏，摺疊如魚鰭

下層，是白水仙中空的莖

冰翅水仙，歌伶水仙，以及

野紫羅蘭暗沉的草葉。諾亞說

憂鬱症患者討厭春天，內在

與外在世界失衡。我的情況

不同──憂鬱，沒錯，但又似乎熱切依戀

有生命的樹，我的身體其實就蜷曲

在分岔的樹幹間，幾乎很平靜

在夜雨中

幾乎能感覺

樹的汁液冒泡，浮昇。諾亞說

認同一棵樹是憂鬱症的

錯亂；喜悅的心

該遊蕩在花園像飄落的葉，是意象的

局部，而非全部

Matins

Unreachable father, when we were first
exiled from heaven, you made
a replica, a place in one sense
different from heaven, being
designed to teach a lesson: otherwise
the same—beauty on either side, beauty
without alternative—Except
we didn't know what was the lesson. Left alone,
we exhausted each other. Years
of darkness followed; we took turns
working the garden, the first tears
filling our eyes as earth
misted with petals, some
dark red, some flesh colored—
We never thought of you
whom we were learning to worship.
We merely knew it wasn't human nature to love
only what returns love.

晨禱

遠不可及的天父啊，當我們初初

被逐出天堂，祢創造了

一個複製品，一個就某種意義而言

異於天堂的地方，讓我們

學些教訓，除此

兩邊就一模一樣：都很美

美得無可選擇——問題是我們

不懂要學甚麼教訓。被孤獨留置著

我們相互耗損。黑暗的年頭

相繼而來；我們輪番

在花園勞動，眼眶滿溢

最初的淚當花瓣如霧

迷漫大地，有些

暗紅，有些染上肉色——

我們從不想念我們曾經學著

去朝拜的祢，只知道

人的天性不會僅僅去愛

那懂得回報愛的

Trillium

When I woke up I was in a forest. The dark
seemed natural, the sky through the pine trees
thick with many lights.

I knew nothing; I could do nothing but see.
And as I watched, all the lights of heaven
faded to make a single thing, a fire
burning through the cool firs.
Then it wasn't possible any longer
to stare at heaven and not be destroyed.

Are there souls that need
death's presence, as I require protection?
I think if I speak long enough
I will answer that question, I will see
whatever they see, a ladder
reaching through the firs, whatever
calls them to exchange their lives—

延齡草

醒來時我在森林。暗
顯得很自然，透過松樹看天空
渾厚，光芒點點

我甚麼都不懂，除了看沒事可做
而當我放眼望去，天上所有的光
褪去，形成單純一團火
穿過沉著的冷杉燃燒
這時就不可能再睜眼
看著上天了，再看就要毀了

是不是有些靈魂需要
死亡示現，一如我需要保護
我想或許我不停說不停說
就能回答這問題，就能看到
他們看到的，那通過冷杉垂懸下的
一把梯子，或那召喚著他們
以生命去交換的不管甚麼──

Think what I understand already.
I woke up ignorant in a forest;
only a moment ago, I didn't know my voice
if one were given to me
would be so full of grief, my sentences
like cries strung together.
I didn't even know I felt grief
until that word came, until I felt
rain streaming from me.

就想一些我懂得的

在森林裡我茫然醒來，僅僅

片刻之前還不了解自己的

聲音（如果我有聲音）

竟如此充滿憂傷，字字句句

像嚎哭聲串連

我甚至不知道自己憂傷

直到憂傷一詞出現，直到我感覺

身體傾洩出　雨

Lamium

This is how you live when you have a cold heart.
As I do: in shadows, trailing over cool rock,
under the great maple trees.

The sun hardly touches me.
Sometimes I see it in early spring, rising very far away.
Then leaves grow over it, completely hiding it. I feel it
glinting through the leaves, erratic,
like someone hitting the side of a glass with a metal spoon.

Living things don't all require
light in the same degree. Some of us
make our own light: a silver leaf
like a path no one can use, a shallow
lake of silver in the darkness under the great maples.

But you know this already.
You and the others who think
you live for truth and, by extension, love
all that is cold.

野芝麻

當你的心是冷的你就會
這麼活，就像我，在陰影
在沉靜的岩石上蔓生，在巨葉楓樹下

太陽幾乎不碰我
早春季節有時我看到它遠遠升起
然後樹葉長滿完全藏住它，我感覺它
透過樹葉閃動，不穩定
彷彿有人拿著金屬湯匙敲玻璃杯

生物不全需要等量的
光照。有些人
自己製造光：一片銀樹葉
像一條小路不為人用，一座淺淺
銀湖在黑暗中在巨葉楓樹下

這情形你早已了然於心——
你，以及那些以為你
為真理而活，進而愛上
那一切冷的

Snowdrops

Do you know what I was, how I lived? You know
what despair is; then
winter should have meaning for you.

I did not expect to survive,
earth suppressing me. I didn't expect
to waken again, to feel
in damp earth my body
able to respond again, remembering
after so long how to open again
in the cold light
of earliest spring—

afraid, yes, but among you again
crying yes risk joy

in the raw wind of the new world.

雪花蓮

你知道我曾經是甚麼我怎麼
活的嗎？你得知道絕望是甚麼
嚴冬對你才有意義

被壓擠在地下
我沒期望能倖存，沒期望
能醒來，在泥濘裡
感覺身體
又有了反應，時隔久遠
竟還能記得如何
開花，在這最初的春日
寒光中──

害怕，是的，能再與你們一起
哭泣我願意以歡愉作注

在這新世界粗糙的風裡

Clear Morning

I've watched you long enough,
I can speak to you any way I like—

I've submitted to your preferences, observing patiently
the things you love, speaking

through vehicles only, in
details of earth, as you prefer,

tendrils
of blue clematis, light,

of early evening—
you would never accept

a voice like mine, indifferent
to the objects you busily name,

your mouths
small circles of awe—

清澈的早晨

我注意你們夠久了
可以對你們暢所欲言——

一向投你們所好，我耐心觀察
你們的偏愛，只透過一些

地表的細節，透過你們偏愛的
媒介表達：比如

藍色鐵線蓮
卷鬚，薄暮的

光——
你們永遠無法接受

我這樣的語氣，對你們
忙碌命名的一切無動於衷

你們把嘴張開
小小的圓圈充滿敬畏——

And all this time
I indulged your limitation, thinking

you would cast it aside yourselves sooner or later,
thinking matter could not absorb your gaze forever—

obstacle of the clematis painting
blue flowers on the porch window—

I cannot go on
restricting myself to images

because you think it is your right
to dispute my meaning:

I am prepared now to force
clarity upon you.

而自始至終
我縱容你們的侷限，以為你們

遲早會放下，以為你們的眼睛
不會永遠陷溺於物質——

那是障礙，比如陽台窗上
鐵線蓮繪出的藍色花朵——

我不能繼續
自囿於形相

因為你們自認有權
質疑我的意義

現在我決定強迫你們
面對真相

Spring Snow

Look at the night sky:
I have two selves, two kinds of power.

I am here with you, at the window,
watching you react. Yesterday
the moon rose over moist earth in the lower garden.
Now the earth glitters like the moon,
like dead matter crusted with light.

You can close your eyes now.
I have heard your cries, and cries before yours,
and the demand behind them.
I have shown you what you want:
not belief, but capitulation
to authority, which depends on violence.

春雪

你注意看夜空：
我有兩個自我，兩種能量

我與你同在，在窗邊
觀察你的反應。昨天
月亮從花園低處濕潤的地面升起
而這時大地閃爍像月亮
像外殼發著光的無生物

這時你可以閉起眼睛了
我已經聽到你以及早於你的那些吶喊
吶喊背後的索求
你想要的我已經展示給你：
不是信服，是屈服
於權威，憑藉暴力的權威

End of Winter

Over the still world, a bird calls
waking solitary among black boughs.

You wanted to be born; I let you be born.
When has my grief ever gotten
in the way of your pleasure?

Plunging ahead
into the dark and light at the same time
eager for sensation

as though you were some new thing, wanting
to express yourselves

all brilliance, all vivacity

never thinking
this would cost you anything,
never imagining the sound of my voice
as anything but part of you—

冬末

靜止的世界之上，一隻鳥
叫哮著，叫醒黑樹枝的孤寂

你們渴望生命，我給你們生命
我的憂傷幾時阻礙了
你們的樂趣？

向前俯衝
同時進入暗與光
渴望某種快感

彷彿你們是新物種，需要
表現自我

光彩洋溢，生氣蓬勃

從不考慮
你們得付出代價
從不想像我的聲音其實
是你們的一部分——

you won't hear it in the other world,
not clearly again,
not in birdcall or human cry,

not the clear sound, only
persistent echoing
in all sound that means good-bye, good-bye—

the one continuous line
that binds us to each other.

這聲音在其他世界你們不會
聽到，不會清楚聽到
不會在鳥鳴或人的呼喚裡

不是清楚的聲音，僅僅
執著地迴響在一切聲音中
暗示著再見，再見——

一條不斷裂的線索
連結著你我

Matins

Forgive me if I say I love you: the powerful
are always lied to since the weak are always
driven by panic. I cannot love
what I can't conceive, and you disclose
virtually nothing: are you like the hawthorn tree,
always the same thing in the same place,
or are you more the foxglove, inconsistent, first springing up
a pink spike on the slope behind the daisies,
and the next year, purple in the rose garden? You must see
it is useless to us, this silence that promotes belief
you must be all things, the foxglove and the hawthorn tree,
the vulnerable rose and tough daisy—we are left to think
you couldn't possibly exist. Is this
what you mean us to think, does this explain
the silence of the morning,
the crickets not yet rubbing their wings, the cats
not fighting in the yard?

晨禱

原諒我如果我說我愛祢：強者

聽到的永遠是謊言，因為弱者永遠

受恐懼驅使。我不能愛

我不瞭解的，而祢幾乎甚麼都

不透露：難道祢像山楂樹

永遠不變在不變的地點

或者祢比較像毛地黃，前後矛盾

先在雛菊後面的坡地長出粉紅穗狀花

第二年變成紫花盛開在玫瑰園？祢一定看出

這對我們沒作用：這樣沉默的推銷

「祢是一切」的信仰，毛地黃和山楂

嬌弱的玫瑰和堅韌的雛菊——我們只能設想

祢不可能存在。這是

祢希望我們想的嗎？是為了

這原因清早才如此安靜：蟋蟀還不

摩擦牠們的翅膀，貓們

在院子裡還不打架？

Matins

I see it is with you as with the birches:
I am not to speak to you
in the personal way. Much
has passed between us. Or
was it always only
on the one side? I am
at fault, at fault, I asked you
to be human—I am no needier
than other people. But the absence
of all feeling, of the least
concern for me—I might as well go on
addressing the birches,
as in my former life: let them
do their worst, let them
bury me with the Romantics,
their pointed yellow leaves
falling and covering me.

晨禱

在我眼裡祢和白樺沒兩樣

我不再用個人方式對祢

說話。祢我之間

發生了不少事。或者

一切永遠只是單面

發生？是我

錯了，我錯了，我要求祢

有人性──我並不比別人

要的更多。但祢欠缺

一切情感，欠缺對我最起碼的

關心──我不如繼續

對這群白樺說話，就像

上輩子那樣：讓它們

盡可能使壞，讓它們

用浪漫主義葬送我，它們

發黃的尖葉子

墜下墜下掩埋我

Scilla

Not I, you idiot, not self, but we, we—waves
of sky blue like
a critique of heaven: why
do you treasure your voice
when to be one thing
is to be next to nothing?
Why do you look up? To hear
an echo like the voice
of god? You are all the same to us,
solitary, standing above us, planning
your silly lives: you go
where you are sent, like all things,
where the wind plants you,
one or another of you forever
looking down and seeing some image
of water, and hearing what? Waves,
and over waves, birds singing.

棉棗兒

不是我，你這傻子，不是個體，是我們，我們 ——
一波波天藍色的浪像是
天堂評論家：你為甚麼還在乎
自己的聲音，如果
是甚麼
幾乎等於甚麼都不是？
你為甚麼還巴望著天空？是想聽到
彷彿上帝口音
的回聲？在我們眼裡，你們全都一個樣
孤伶伶站在我們上方規畫
你們的傻日子：去
被送去的地方，就像世間萬物
隨風栽種
你們其中某個人會一直往下
探視，看見一些水的意象
然後聽到，甚麼？一波波浪
波浪上，群鳥不停地唱

Retreating Wind

When I made you, I loved you.
Now I pity you.

I gave you all you needed:
bed of earth, blanket of blue air—

As I get further away from you
I see you more clearly.
Your souls should have been immense by now,
not what they are,
small talking things—

I gave you every gift,
blue of the spring morning,
time you didn't know how to use—
you wanted more, the one gift
reserved for another creation.

Whatever you hoped,
you will not find yourselves in the garden,

退隱的風

創造你們之初，我愛你們
現在我憐憫你們

我給了你們一切所需：
大地為床，藍天為氈——

離你們愈遠
我愈看清你們
你們的靈魂這時該十分壯闊
不該是這樣
瑣碎嚼舌的東西

我給了你們一切：
春天早晨的藍
你們不知如何善用的時光——
而你們想要更多，想要那件
保留給其他造物的禮

不管你們多麼渴望
你們不會在花園繁茂的植物間

among the growing plants.

Your lives are not circular like theirs:

your lives are the bird's flight
which begins and ends in stillness—
which *begins* and *ends*, in form echoing
this arc from the white birch
to the apple tree.

找到自己；不像
植物，你們的生命不循環

你們的生命是鳥之飛翔
始於靜止，終於靜止——
有始，有終，那模式恰巧反映著
白樺到蘋果樹間的弧形

The Garden

I couldn't do it again,
I can hardly bear to look at it—

in the garden, in light rain
the young couple planting
a row of peas, as though
no one has ever done this before,
the great difficulties have never as yet
been faced and solved—

They cannot see themselves,
in fresh dirt, starting up
without perspective,
the hills behind them pale green, clouded with flowers—

She wants to stop;
he wants to get to the end,
to stay with the thing—

Look at her, touching his cheek
to make a truce, her fingers

花園

看不下去了
我不忍心再看下去──

細雨花園裡
那對年輕夫妻正在栽種
一排豌豆，彷彿
這是一項創舉
沒有人曾經面對或解決過
這麼大的難題──

他們看不到自己
在一片爛泥地，初步動工
看不透全貌
背後是灰綠山丘，花朵覆蓋如雲──

她想停下來
他想堅持
到底──

看看她！撫摸他的面頰
休戰，她的手指冰冷

cool with spring rain;

in thin grass, bursts of purple crocus—

even here, even at the beginning of love,

her hand leaving his face makes

an image of departure

and they think

they are free to overlook

this sadness.

沾著春雨
稀疏的草地冒出紫色番紅花——

就算在這裡，在這愛的起點
她的手離開他臉龐，已然
留下一個分手的意象

而他們以為
他們可以忽視
這悲哀

The Hawthorn Tree

Side by side, not

hand in hand: I watch you

walking in the summer garden—things

that can't move

learn to see; I do not need

to chase you through

the garden; human beings leave

signs of feeling

everywhere, flowers

scattered on the dirt path, all

white and gold, some

lifted a little by

the evening wind; I do not need

to follow where you are now,

deep in the poisonous field, to know

the cause of your flight, human

passion or rage: for what else

would you let drop

all you have gathered?

山楂

並行而不

牽手：我看著你們

在夏日花園走動──

不能動的要學會用眼睛

看；我不必穿越花園

追逐你，人類總是四處留下

感情的痕跡，花

四處散落泥徑，滿地

粉白金黃，有些

被晚風稍微

掀動；我不必隨你深入

那片毒草原，到你

目前所在，以了解你飛奔而逃

是為激情

或憤怒，因為除此

還有甚麼能讓你拋下

已經採集在手的一切呢？

Love in Moonlight

Sometimes a man or woman forces his despair
on another person, which is called
baring the heart, alternatively, baring the soul—
meaning for this moment they acquired souls—
outside, a summer evening, a whole world
thrown away on the moon: groups of silver forms
which might be buildings or trees, the narrow garden
where the cat hides, rolling on its back in the dust,
the rose, the coreopsis, and, in the dark, the gold
    dome of the capitol
converted to an alloy of moonlight, shape
without detail, the myth, the archetype, the soul
filled with fire that is moonlight really, taken
from another source, and briefly
shining as the moon shines: stone or not,
the moon is still that much of a living thing.

愛在月光下

男人女人有時把自己的絕望

強加於另一人，說是

袒露心思，或靈魂告白──

表示這一刻他們有了靈魂──

外面，是夏夜，整個世界

都耗在月亮上：一群群銀色形體

可能是建築或樹，躲在狹窄花園的

貓翻滾著，背脊摩擦塵土

玫瑰，孔雀菊，黑暗中金色的

　　　議會大廈圓頂

轉化成月光合金，有形狀

沒有細節，神話，原型，靈魂

充滿了火其實是月光，來自

另一個源頭，短暫發光

像月亮發光：不管是不是石頭

月亮仍然多少是個活體

April

No one's despair is like my despair—

You have no place in this garden
thinking such things, producing
the tiresome outward signs; the man
pointedly weeding an entire forest,
the woman limping, refusing to change clothes
or wash her hair.

Do you suppose I care
if you speak to one another?
But I mean you to know
I expected better of two creatures
who were given minds: if not
that you would actually care for each other
at least that you would understand
grief is distributed
between you, among all your kind, for me
to know you, as deep blue

四月

沒有誰像我一樣絕望——

這花園沒有你思考
這些事的餘地，製造些累人的
表面訊息：男人
徒勞地為整片森林除草
女人拖著腳走，拒絕換衣服
拒絕洗頭

你以為
我會在乎你們
相互說不說話？但我要你知道
我對兩個理性動物
是有期待的：就算你們
實際不再關心對方
至少也該了解
在你們之間，在所有你們的同類
之間，我散播了憂傷以便
能認出你們，就像深藍

marks the wild scilla, white
the wood violet.

烙印在棉棗兒，白
之於野菫

Violets

Because in our world
something is always hidden,
small and white,
small and what you call
pure, we do not grieve
as you grieve, dear
suffering master; you
are no more lost
than we are, under
the hawthorn tree, the hawthorn holding
balanced trays of pearls: what
has brought you among us
who would teach you, though
you kneel and weep,
clasping your great hands,
in all your greatness knowing
nothing of the soul's nature,
which is never to die: poor sad god,
either you never have one
or you never lose one.

野菫

因為在我們的世界

有些東西永遠隱藏著

微小且白

微小而（按你的

說法）純潔，我們不像你

一樣傷感，親愛的

受苦受難的主人，你

並不比我們

更迷惘，在山楂樹下

山楂樹捧著一盤盤

勻稱的珍珠：是甚麼

引你前來這裡

要我們開導你，雖然

你跪著，哭泣

緊握你能幹的手

優越如你卻對靈魂

永恆不死的本質一無所知

可憐憂傷的主子啊

要不你從來就沒有靈魂，要不

你永遠也不會失去它

Witchgrass

Something
comes into the world unwelcome
calling disorder, disorder—

If you hate me so much
don't bother to give me
a name: do you need
one more slur
in your language, another
way to blame
one tribe for everything—

as we both know,
if you worship
one god, you only need
one enemy—

I'm not the enemy.
Only a ruse to ignore
what you see happening
right here in this bed,

巫草

有些東西來到世間
卻惹人嫌
召來混亂，混亂——

如果你那麼恨我
就別費神替我
取名字：難道你需要
語言裡多添一個
含糊的嘟囔，需要
另一種方式
找一隻替罪羔羊——

我們都了解
如果你信
一個神，你只需要
一個敵人——

我不是敵人，只是
一個障眼法，好讓你忽視
發生在這裡
在這床上的事

a little paradigm
of failure. One of your precious flowers
dies here almost every day
and you can't rest until
you attack the cause, meaning
whatever is left, whatever
happens to be sturdier
than your personal passion—

It was not meant
to last forever in the real world.
But why admit that, when you can go on
doing what you always do,
mourning and laying blame,
always the two together.

I don't need your praise
to survive. I was here first,
before you were here, before
you ever planted a garden.
And I'll be here when only the sun and moon
are left, and the sea, and the wide field.

I will constitute the field.

一個失敗的
小小範例。你珍愛的花
幾乎一天死一棵
你無法心安除非
抓到元兇，箭頭這就指向
那剩下的，恰巧
比你個人所偏愛
更頑強的那些——

現世的一切
原不為永存不朽
但何必這麼承認如果你能
繼續你一貫的
做法：哀悼和委過
永遠秤不離砣

不需要你歌頌
我也能生存。我是最先來的
比你先，先於你
耕作這花園之始
而我會留在這，直到只剩
太陽和月亮，以及海，以及曠野

我會統領這野地

The Jacob's Ladder

Trapped in the earth,
wouldn't you too want to go
to heaven? I live
in a lady's garden. Forgive me, lady;
longing has taken my grace. I am
not what you wanted. But
as men and women seem
to desire each other, I too desire
knowledge of paradise—and now
your grief, a naked stem
reaching the porch window.
And at the end, what? A small blue flower
like a star. Never
to leave the world! Is this
not what your tears mean?

雅各之梯・花蔥

受困土壤裡

難道你不會同樣想要

上天堂？我活在

一位女士的花園。抱歉了女士

因為渴望，我不再優雅

辜負了你的期待。但就像

男女似乎相互吸引，伊甸園的

知識也吸引著我——而現在

你的悲傷是一截花梗赤裸裸

伸到陽台窗口。結果

又如何？一朵藍色小花

像一顆星。永遠

不得脫離這世界！這不正是你

淚水的意涵？

Matins

You want to know how I spend my time?
I walk the front lawn, pretending
to be weeding. You ought to know
I'm never weeding, on my knees, pulling
clumps of clover from the flower beds: in fact
I'm looking for courage, for some evidence
my life will change, though
it takes forever, checking
each clump for the symbolic
leaf, and soon the summer is ending, already
the leaves turning, always the sick trees
going first, the dying turning
brilliant yellow, while a few dark birds perform
their curfew of music. You want to see my hands?
As empty now as at the first note.
Or was the point always
to continue without a sign?

晨禱

祢想知道我怎麼打發時間？
在前院草坪上走動，假裝
除草。祢一定知道
我從來沒在除草，跪著，從花圃
拔起一叢叢苜蓿我其實
是在找勇氣，找一些跡象
證明我的生命會改變，檢查
每株苜蓿找一片有象徵意味的
葉子，雖然進展
曠日廢時，而夏天很快就結束了
樹葉已經變色，生病的樹永遠最先
落葉，瀕死的葉子黃燦燦的
幾隻黑鳥這時唱著牠們的宵禁
之歌。祢想看我的手？手
這時是空的，就像那最初的單音
重點或許就在這：永遠
繼續下去，不會有兆示？

Matins

What is my heart to you
that you must break it over and over
like a plantsman testing
his new species? Practice
on something else: how can I live
in colonies, as you prefer, if you impose
a quarantine of affliction, dividing me
from healthy members of
my own tribe: you do not do this
in the garden, segregate
the sick rose; you let it wave its sociable
infested leaves in
the faces of other roses, and the tiny aphids
leap from plant to plant, proving yet again
I am the lowest of your creatures, following
the thriving aphid and the trailing rose— Father,
as agent of my solitude, alleviate
at least my guilt; lift
the stigma of isolation, unless
it is your plan to make me
sound forever again, as I was
sound and whole in my mistaken childhood,

晨禱

對祢，我的心到底是甚麼

需要祢一次次弄碎它

像園藝家試驗

新品種？祢就試驗些別的吧

我怎麼可能如祢所願

活在殖民地，如果祢非要

設立一個疫區隔離我

和我健康的同類。在花園

祢不會這樣隔離

害病的玫瑰，祢讓它

對著其他玫瑰舞動它氾濫的

善交際的葉子，讓小蚜蟲活躍

在玫瑰和玫瑰間：這恰恰證明

我是祢最低等的造物，低於

旺盛的蚜蟲和蔓枝玫瑰——天父啊

作為我孤獨的起因，請祢至少

減輕我的罪惡感，消除

這隔離之恥，除非祢計畫

讓我再次永遠健康

健康而完整一如

or if not then, under the light weight

of my mother's heart, or if not then

in dream, first

being that would never die.

在我錯誤的童年，要不
一如在我母親飄忽的
心裡，或者要不
就在夢中，最起碼
夢永遠不死

Song

Like a protected heart,
the blood-red
flower of the wild rose begins
to open on the lowest branch,
supported by the netted
mass of a large shrub:
it blooms against the dark
which is the heart's constant
backdrop, while flowers
higher up have wilted or rotted;
to survive
adversity merely
deepens its color. But John
objects, he thinks
if this were not a poem but
an actual garden, then
the red rose would be
required to resemble
nothing else, neither
another flower nor
the shadowy heart, at

歌

像一顆受保護的心

血紅的

野玫瑰從花梗最低處

開始開花

龐大的網狀灌木叢

是它的支撐

襯托著花的

暗色調，是那顆心不變的

背景，這時高處的花

已經枯萎或腐爛

倖存

在逆境

只讓它的色澤更深沉。但約翰

不以為然，他覺得

如果這不是一首詩而是

實際的花園

紅玫瑰就不必

和其他東西類比，不必是

另一種花

不必是陰影籠罩的心

earth level pulsing
half maroon, half crimson.

在與土壤等高處

它顫動著

半是暗紅，半鮮紅

Field Flowers

What are you saying? That you want
eternal life? Are your thoughts really
as compelling as all that? Certainly
you don't look at us, don't listen to us,
on your skin
stain of sun, dust
of yellow buttercups: I'm talking
to you, you staring through
bars of high grass shaking
your little rattle— O
the soul! the soul! Is it enough
only to look inward? Contempt
for humanity is one thing, but why
disdain the expansive
field, your gaze rising over the clear heads
of the wild buttercups into what? Your poor
idea of heaven: absence
of change. Better than earth? How
would you know, who are neither
here nor there, standing in our midst?

野花

你說甚麼？希望生命
不死？你的想法
都這麼驚人嗎？顯然
你沒看我們也沒聽我們
你皮膚上沾著
太陽的汗痕，金黃
禺毛茛的粉塵，我正對你說話
而你的眼光穿透野草
高聳的柵欄，晃動你的
撥浪鼓喋喋著──噢
靈魂！靈魂！難道單單
往內看就夠了？輕忽人
是一回事，但為甚麼
藐視這寬闊的原野
越過禺毛茛純淨的花冠
你凝視甚麼？你貧乏的
天堂概念啊：一成
不變。它比地球好？站在
我們中間，既不在彼也不在此
你如何知道？

The Red Poppy

The great thing
is not having
a mind. Feelings:
oh, I have those; they
govern me. I have
a lord in heaven
called the sun, and open
for him, showing him
the fire of my own heart, fire
like his presence.
What could such glory be
if not a heart? Oh my brothers and sisters,
were you like me once, long ago,
before you were human? Did you
permit yourselves
to open once, who would never
open again? Because in truth
I am speaking now
the way you do. I speak
because I am shattered.

紅罌粟

最好是

沒有

心思。而感覺

噢，我有很多感覺，感覺

統治我。我有

一個主人在天上

名叫太陽，我為他

開放，向他披露我

內心的火，形貌一如他的

火

而如此輝煌的，不是心

又能是甚麼？噢我的兄弟姊妹

許久以前，在成為人類之前，你們

是否曾經和我一樣

是否曾經允許永遠無法

花開二度的自己

開放那麼一次？因為事實上

此刻，一如你們

我正在說話。我開口說話

因為我已經碎成片片

Clover

What is dispersed
among us, which you call
the sign of blessedness
although it is, like us,
a weed, a thing
to be rooted out—

by what logic
do you hoard
a single tendril
of something you want
dead?

If there is any presence among us
so powerful, should it not
multiply, in service
of the adored garden?

You should be asking
these questions yourself,
not leaving them

苜蓿

散置在
我們中間，你說是
幸運預兆的，其實
就像我們，也是雜草
遲早要被連根
拔掉——

到底憑甚麼邏輯
你要蒐藏這
來自你企圖消滅之物的
單獨一根
鬚莖？

我同類之中若有誰展現出
任何超能力
難道不該讓它量化
為這迷人的花園奉獻？

這些問題你該
問自己，不要問

to your victims. You should know

that when you swagger among us

I hear two voices speaking,

one your spirit, one

the acts of your hands.

你的受害者。你該知道
當你闊步在我們當中
我聽到兩種聲音：其一
來自你的心
其二，你雙手的動作

Matins

Not the sun merely but the earth
itself shines, white fire
leaping from the showy mountains
and the flat road
shimmering in early morning: is this
for us only, to induce
response, or are you
stirred also, helpless
to control yourself
in earth's presence— I am ashamed
at what I thought you were,
distant from us, regarding us
as an experiment: it is
a bitter thing to be
the disposable animal,
a bitter thing. Dear friend,
dear trembling partner, what
surprises you most in what you feel,
earth's radiance or your own delight?
For me, always
the delight is the surprise.

晨禱

不只太陽，地球

自體也會發光，白色火焰

從醒目的山頭躍出

平坦的道路

在大清早閃爍：這一切

只為我們，為引起我們的反應

而發生嗎？或者祢也同樣

感覺騷動，為大地的風采

亢奮不已——真慚愧

我誤解了祢

以為祢疏遠我們

拿我們當試驗：作為可拋式

一次性的不堪動物

是件不堪的事。親愛的朋友

顫抖的親密夥伴啊

祢最意外的感受是這

大地的燦爛或是祢自身的喜悅？

對我，向來

喜悅就是一種意外

Heaven and Earth

Where one finishes, the other begins.
On top, a band of blue; underneath,
a band of green and gold, green and deep rose.

John stands at the horizon: he wants
both at once, he wants
everything at once.

The extremes are easy. Only
the middle is a puzzle. Midsummer—
everything is possible.

Meaning: never again will life end.

How can I leave my husband
standing in the garden
dreaming this sort of thing, holding
his rake, triumphantly
preparing to announce this discovery

天與地

一邊結束，另一邊就開始
上面，一整片藍；下面
是鎏金快綠，綠與玫瑰暗紅

約翰站在地平線上
他兩邊都要，同時要
他想同時得到一切

極端的兩邊還單純
中間地帶卻混亂。仲夏時期
一切都有無限可能

換言之：生命自此永無休止

我怎能放任我的丈夫
站在花園
手握鋤耙幻想著
這類事情，意氣風發地
準備宣告這新發現

as the fire of the summer sun
truly does stall
being entirely contained by
the burning maples
at the garden's border.

而夏日的火焰

這時確實也留了下來

花園周邊

一群燃燒的楓樹

團團包圍著它

The Doorway

I wanted to stay as I was
still as the world is never still,
not in midsummer but the moment before
the first flower forms, the moment
nothing is as yet past—

not midsummer, the intoxicant,
but late spring, the grass not yet
high at the edge of the garden, the early tulips
beginning to open—

like a child hovering in a doorway, watching the others,
the ones who go first,
a tense cluster of limbs, alert to
the failures of others, the public falterings

with a child's fierce confidence of imminent power
preparing to defeat
these weaknesses, to succumb
to nothing, the time directly

門口

我想停下來，像以往一樣
靜止，因為世界從來不靜止
不停在仲夏，而停在第一朵花
成形之前，一切還沒過去
那一刻——

不停在迷醉的仲夏
而停在晚春，花園周邊
野草還沒抽高，早熟的鬱金香
開始綻放——

像一個孩子徘徊門口，看著
那些跑得最快的
手忙腳亂推擠一團，警覺
他們的失誤，眾目下的畏縮踉蹌

帶著孩子對能量爆發的強烈
信心，準備好去克服
這些弱點，不對任何事
低頭，恰恰是

prior to flowering, the epoch of mastery

before the appearance of the gift,
before possession.

花開前那一刻，掌握自如的時期

在天賦顯現之前
在擁有之前

Midsummer

How can I help you when you all want
different things–sunlight and shadow,
moist darkness, dry heat—

Listen to yourselves, vying with one another—

And you wonder
why I despair of you,
you think something could fuse you into a whole—

the still air of high summer
tangled with a thousand voices

each calling out
some need, some absolute

and in that name continually
strangling each other
in the open field—

仲夏

我怎能幫得了你們如果
你們的需求各個不同
日照，陰影，濕暗，乾熱——

你們自己聽聽，爭先恐後的——

而你們還納悶
為甚麼我對你們絕望，以為
有甚麼能助你們結合為一

盛夏沉寂的空氣
糾纏著一千種聲音

每個聲音都高喊著
一些需要，一些必要

並且藉此不斷
相互扼殺
在開闊的原野——

For what? For space and air?
The privilege of being
single in the eyes of heaven?

You were not intended
to be unique. You were
my embodiment, all diversity

not what you think you see
searching the bright sky over the field,
your incidental souls
fixed like telescopes on some
enlargement of yourselves—

Why would I make you if I meant
to limit myself
to the ascendant sign,
the star, the fire, the fury?

這是為甚麼？為空間和
空氣？為獨佔老天爺
眷顧的特權？

但我並沒打算給你們
獨特性。你們是我的
體現，千變萬化，不是你們

搜索著原野晴空時
自以為見到的
你們偶然附帶的靈魂
像望遠鏡，固定在你們某種
放大的自我上——

如果我有意以優越的
表象：星星，火，狂風暴雨
侷限住自己
我又何必創造你們？

Vespers

Once I believed in you; I planted a fig tree.
Here, in Vermont, country
of no summer. It was a test: if the tree lived,
it would mean you existed.

By this logic, you do not exist. Or you exist
exclusively in warmer climates,
in fervent Sicily and Mexico and California,
where are grown the unimaginable
apricot and fragile peach. Perhaps
they see your face in Sicily; here we barely see
the hem of your garment. I have to discipline myself
to share with John and Noah the tomato crop.

If there is justice in some other world, those
like myself, whom nature forces
into lives of abstinence, should get
the lion's share of all things, all
objects of hunger, greed being
praise of you. And no one praises

晚禱

我曾經信過祢：種了一棵無花果樹
在這裡，在佛蒙特，一個
沒有夏天的地方。那是個試探：如果樹
活了，表示祢存在

按照這邏輯祢就不存在。或者祢
單單只存在溫暖氣候帶
在熱情的西西里，墨西哥，加利福尼亞
那邊也長著不可思議的
杏子和嬌滴滴的水蜜桃。也許
人們在西西里能見到祢的臉，但在這
我們幾乎連祢的衣襬都看不到。我很勉強
才捨得把收成的番茄分給諾亞和約翰

如果另一個世界有正義，那些像我
一樣被大自然逼迫著
節省度日的人，就該得到所有
抗饑荒農作物的
最大一份，因為貪欲
是祢讚賞的，而沒有人比我

more intensely than I, with more

painfully checked desire, or more deserves

to sit at your right hand, if it exists, partaking

of the perishable, the immortal fig,

which does not travel.

更認真地歌頌貪欲，比我有更多痛苦

檢驗過的欲望，比我更配

坐在祢右手邊（如果祢有手）分享

那容易腐爛，不朽的

不移動大駕的無花果

Vespers

In your extended absence, you permit me
use of earth, anticipating
some return on investment. I must report
failure in my assignment, principally
regarding the tomato plants.
I think I should not be encouraged to grow
tomatoes. Or, if I am, you should withhold
the heavy rains, the cold nights that come
so often here, while other regions get
twelve weeks of summer. All this
belongs to you: on the other hand,
I planted the seeds, I watched the first shoots
like wings tearing the soil, and it was my heart
broken by the blight, the black spot so quickly
multiplying in the rows. I doubt
you have a heart, in our understanding of
that term. You who do not discriminate
between the dead and the living, who are, in consequence,
immune to foreshadowing, you may not know
how much terror we bear, the spotted leaf,
the red leaves of the maple falling

晚禱

在祢長期缺席中，祢允許我

使用大地，預計能得到

一些投資報酬。我必須向祢報告

我的任務失敗了，主要是

因為番茄。我想

我不該被鼓動著去種番茄，或者

如果我真被鼓動了，你該禁止

那些豪雨，那些寒夜，它們

來得太勤了，而別處每年

卻有十二個禮拜的夏天。這裡的一切

都是祢的，但從另一角度來看

種子是我種下的，我看著初生幼苗

翅膀般破土而出，而當枯死病

黑色的斑點一排排迅速繁殖

我的心都碎了。我懷疑

祢到底有沒有心，那種我們認知的

心。對生死一視同仁

因此不受惡兆干擾的祢，也許不了解

我們承受了多少驚嚇：葉子長出斑點

紅楓葉片片飄落甚至在八月

even in August, in early darkness: I am responsible
for these vines.

在早來的黑夜：對這些番茄藤

我是有責任的啊

Vespers

More than you love me, very possibly
you love the beasts of the field, even,
possibly, the field itself, in August dotted
with wild chicory and aster:
I know. I have compared myself
to those flowers, their range of feeling
so much smaller and without issue; also to white sheep,
actually gray: I am uniquely
suited to praise you. Then why
torment me? I study the hawkweed,
the buttercup protected from the grazing herd
by being poisonous: is pain
your gift to make me
conscious in my need of you, as though
I must need you to worship you,
or have you abandoned me
in favor of the field, the stoic lambs turning
silver in twilight; waves of wild aster and chicory shining
pale blue and deep blue, since you already know
how like your raiment it is.

晚禱

勝過愛我，祢很可能更愛

原野的走獸，或甚至八月裡

點綴著野菊苣和紫菀的原野

本身──這我明白

我拿自己和那些野草花比較過

它們感知範圍小得多

也沒有判斷力；我也比較過

白綿羊（其實是灰色）：我該是

讚頌祢的最佳人選。那麼

祢為甚麼折磨我？我研究過山柳菊

和毛茛，牛羊不吃它們

因為它們有毒：痛苦

難道是祢賜給我的恩典

好讓我意識到我需要祢？似乎為了

信奉祢，我必須需要祢

或任祢遺棄我，去袒護那片原野

那群在微曦中發出銀亮光的

斯多葛學派羔羊；一波波野紫菀和菊苣

閃著淡藍深藍，因為祢早就知道

那藍色多麼肖似祢的衣著

Daisies

Go ahead: say what you're thinking. The garden
is not the real world. Machines
are the real world. Say frankly what any fool
could read in your face: it makes sense
to avoid us, to resist
nostalgia. It is
not modern enough, the sound the wind makes
stirring a meadow of daisies: the mind
cannot shine following it. And the mind
wants to shine, plainly, as
machines shine, and not
grow deep, as, for example, roots. It is very touching,
all the same, to see you cautiously
approaching the meadow's border in early morning,
when no one could possibly
be watching you. The longer you stand at the edge,
the more nervous you seem. No one wants to hear
impressions of the natural world: you will be
laughed at again; scorn will be piled on you.
As for what you're actually

雛菊

說吧,你在想甚麼就直說:花園
不是真實世界。機械的
世界才真實。你就坦白說出
連呆子都能從你臉上讀到的這種
想法;避開我們,抗拒懷舊
很合理。說甚麼
風聲攪動了整片雛菊的原野
這都落伍了;跟著這調調
心智沒法發光發亮
而心智渴望發光發亮
很簡單,像機械發光發亮
不像植物生根,往深處長
但在四下無人的清早看見你
躡手躡腳走近草原
邊界,仍然讓人感動
在邊界站得愈久
你愈顯得慌張,沒有人想聽
你對大自然的感受,你會被訕笑
會有一堆冷眼等著你——
至於今天早晨在這曠野

hearing this morning: think twice

before you tell anyone what was said in this field

and by whom.

你確實聽見

有誰對你說了些甚麼

要告訴任何人之前你還是多想想吧

End of Summer

After all things occurred to me,
the void occurred to me.

There is a limit
to the pleasure I had in form—

I am not like you in this,
I have no release in another body,

I have no need
of shelter outside myself—

My poor inspired
creation, you are
distractions, finally,
mere curtailment; you are
too little like me in the end
to please me.

And so adamant—
you want to be paid off

夏末

一切都發生過後
空虛出現了

表象能帶給我的喜悅
是有限的

這方面我不像你
我從不寄情於另一種形體

我不需要任何
身外的庇護——

我可憐的受到啟蒙的
造物啊，你終究是
一種干擾，只能草草
收尾；跟我一樣
你過於渺小，到底
無法取悅我

而且你非常頑固——
臨走還要索討

for your disappearance,
all paid in some part of the earth,
some souvenir, as you were once
rewarded for labor,
the scribe being paid
in silver, the shepherd in barley

although it is not earth
that is lasting, not
these small chips of matter—

If you would open your eyes
you would see me, you would see
the emptiness of heaven
mirrored on earth, the fields
vacant again, lifeless, covered with snow—

then white light
no longer disguised as matter.

遣散費

拿走大地的一部分

拿走一些紀念，就像你曾經

從工作獲得酬勞

就像繕寫員得到銀子

牧羊人得到麥子

雖然可長可久的

不是大地，也不是

這些瑣碎物質

如果你願意睜開眼

就會看見我，就會看見

天堂的空虛

反映在大地，原野再次

一無所有一無生息，覆蓋著雪——

然後，白煞煞的光

不再偽裝成物質

Vespers

I don't wonder where you are anymore.
You're in the garden; you're where John is,
in the dirt, abstracted, holding his green trowel.
This is how he gardens: fifteen minutes of intense effort,
fifteen minutes of ecstatic contemplation. Sometimes
I work beside him, doing the shade chores,
weeding, thinning the lettuces; sometimes I watch
from the porch near the upper garden until twilight makes
lamps of the first lilies: all this time,
peace never leaves him. But it rushes through me,
not as sustenance the flower holds
but like bright light through the bare tree.

晚禱

我不再納悶祢到底在哪了

祢就在花園，跟約翰在一起

在爛泥地，抽離的，拿著他的鏟子——

約翰是這麼做園藝的：十五分鐘密集工作

十五鐘出神思考。有時候

我就在他身邊做些閒差

拔草，為萵苣分株；有時我會從

上層花園旁的陽台望去，直到黃昏點燃

第一叢百合。這整個期間

約翰永遠很平靜，但對我，平靜

稍縱即逝，不像花能儲存養分

而像一道閃光穿透光禿的樹

Vespers

Even as you appeared to Moses, because
I need you, you appear to me, not
often, however. I live essentially
in darkness. You are perhaps training me to be
responsive to the slightest brightening. Or, like the poets,
are you stimulated by despair, does grief
move you to reveal your nature? This afternoon,
in the physical world to which you commonly
contribute your silence, I climbed
the small hill above the wild blueberries, metaphysically
descending, as on all my walks: did I go deep enough
for you to pity me, as you have sometimes pitied
others who suffer, favoring those
with theological gifts? As you anticipated,
I did not look up. So you came down to me:
at my feet, not the wax
leaves of the wild blueberry but your fiery self, a whole
pasture of fire, and beyond, the red sun neither falling
            nor rising—
I was not a child; I could take advantage of illusions.

晚禱

就算祢現身我眼前（雖然這事
難得發生）如同祢現身摩西眼前
因為我需要祢，本質上我還是活在
黑暗中。也許祢是要鍛鍊我
讓我對最弱的光也能反應；或者
祢像詩人，絕望能激發祢而憂傷
能觸動祢讓祢展露天性？今天下午
在祢一貫保持沉默的
這物質世界，我越過野藍莓叢
爬上一座小山丘，形而上的
往下走，就像每一次散步。我走得
是否夠深是否足以博取祢憐憫
一如祢憐憫其他受苦的人，尤其其中
有神學稟賦的那些？不出祢預料
我並不往天上看，所以祢下來
找我：我腳下，不是蠟質的野藍莓葉
而是火爆的祢，一整片牧場
全是火，火紅的太陽不上不下懸在半空——
我不是小孩，幻覺對我有好處

Vespers

You thought we didn't know. But we knew once,
children know these things. Don't turn away now—
    we inhabited
a lie to appease you. I remember
sunlight of early spring, embankments
netted with dark vinca. I remember
lying in a field, touching my brother's body.
Don't turn away now; we denied
memory to console you. We mimicked you, reciting
the terms of our punishment. I remember
some of it, not all of it: deceit
begins as forgetting. I remember small things, flowers
growing under the hawthorn tree, bells
of the wild scilla. Not all, but enough
to know you exist: who else had reason to create
mistrust between a brother and sister but the one
who profited, to whom we turned in solitude? Who else
would so envy the bond we had then
as to tell us it was not earth
but heaven we were losing?

晚禱

祢以為我們不懂。我們懂的
這種事小孩子全懂。祢別掉頭走——
我們只是撒了謊好讓祢安心
我還記得早春的陽光，河堤長滿
深色日日春；我記得
躺在野地觸摸我哥的身體——
別走開啊祢現在。為了安撫祢
我們否定記憶，模仿祢，熟背祢的
懲罰條例；我記得其中一些
但不記得全部：欺騙
始於遺忘。我記得一些瑣事
山楂樹下的花，野棉棗兒的鈴鐺
不記得全部，但多得足夠
知道祢存在：還有誰有理由製造
兄妹間的猜疑，除了在孤單中
我們轉而求助因而漁翁得利的那一位
還有誰會如此忌妒我們
曾經擁有的親密而宣稱
我們失去的不是人間，是天堂？

Early Darkness

How can you say
earth should give me joy? Each thing
born is my burden; I cannot succeed
with all of you.

And you would like to dictate to me,
you would like to tell me
who among you is most valuable,
who most resembles me.
And you hold up as an example
the pure life, the detachment
you struggle to achieve—

How can you understand me
when you cannot understand yourselves?
Your memory is not
powerful enough, it will not
reach back far enough—

初闇

你們怎麼能說
大地帶給我快樂？每一個生命
都是我的負擔；對你們
我不是都有辦法

而且你們總想支使我
想要我知道你們當中
誰最有價值
誰最像我
然後舉例證明
你們如何掙扎著過清教徒日子
離群索居──

你們如何能了解我
如果連自己都不了解
你們的記性不夠
強，追溯得不夠深
不夠遠──

Never forget you are my children.

You are not suffering because you touched each other

but because you were born,

because you required life

separate from me.

永遠別忘了你們是我的孩子

你們痛苦不是因為你們相互觸碰

而是因為你們有了生命

因為你們要求

獨立於我的生命

Harvest

It grieves me to think of you in the past—

Look at you, blindly clinging to earth
as though it were the vineyards of heaven
while the fields go up in flames around you—

Ah, little ones, how unsubtle you are:
it is at once the gift and the torment.

If what you fear in death
is punishment beyond this, you need not
fear death:

how many times must I destroy my own creation
to teach you
this is your punishment:

with one gesture I established you
in time and in paradise.

收成

想到你們的經歷我就難過

看看你們，盲目地黏貼著土地
以為它是天堂的葡萄園
而田野裡火勢正洶洶環繞——

小傢伙們，你們真遲鈍啊
這片土地它是恩賜同時也是折磨

如果你們害怕死亡
是這之後的懲罰，你們就不必
怕死

而我到底要把我的作物
毀掉多少次，你們才明白
這，就是你們的懲罰：曾經

我以一個手勢，置你們於
時間，於伊甸

The White Rose

This is the earth? Then
I don't belong here.

Who are you in the lighted window,
shadowed now by the flickering leaves
of the wayfarer tree?
Can you survive where I won't last
beyond the first summer?

All night the slender branches of the tree
shift and rustle at the bright window.
Explain my life to me, you who make no sign,

though I call out to you in the night:
I am not like you, I have only
my body for a voice; I can't
disappear into silence—

And in the cold morning
over the dark surface of the earth

白玫瑰

這是人間？如果是
我就不屬於這兒

而你又是誰，在亮著燈的
窗裡？窗
這時被莢蒾閃爍的葉子
遮掩住。你活得過我活不過的
這第一個夏季嗎？

一整夜莢蒾瘦長的枝椏
對著發亮的窗窸窣搖曳。請為我
解釋一下我的生命吧，夜深了

我向你求助你卻毫無動靜
我不像你，我只有
這一具身體可以發聲，我不能
消失於沉默——

而在這冷冷清晨
昏暗的地表之上

echoes of my voice drift,
whiteness steadily absorbed into darkness

as though you were making a sign after all
to convince me you too couldn't survive here

or to show me you are not the light I called to
but the blackness behind it.

我的聲音迴盪飄散，持續地
白色沒入黑色，彷彿

你終於給了暗示，要我相信
你在這裡也無法生存，或者表明

你不是我求助的那道光
而是它背後的陰影

Ipomoea

What was my crime in another life,
as in this life my crime
is sorrow, that I am not to be
permitted to ascend ever again,
never in any sense
permitted to repeat my life,
wound in the hawthorn, all
earthly beauty my punishment
as it is yours—
Source of my suffering, why
have you drawn from me
these flowers like the sky, except
to mark me as a part
of my master: I am
his cloak's color, my flesh giveth
form to his glory.

朝顏

譬如這輩子
憂傷是我的罪，上輩子
我到底犯了甚麼錯使得我
永世不得超脫
就任何意義而言永遠
無法重複我的生命
纏繞著山楂樹，一切世間的
美對我都是懲罰
一如對你——
我痛苦的源頭啊，你
為甚麼要從我身上扯出
這些貌似藍天的花，除非
為了標示我是我主子的
一部分：我是祂
罩袍的顏色，我的肉身
具現了祂的華美

Presque Isle

In every life, there's a moment or two.
In every life, a room somewhere, by the sea or
      in the mountains.

On the table, a dish of apricots. Pits in a white ashtray.

Like all images, these were the conditions of a pact:
on your cheek, tremor of sunlight,
my finger pressing your lips.
The walls blue-white; paint from the low bureau
      flaking a little.

That room must still exist, on the fourth floor,
with a small balcony overlooking the ocean.
A square white room, the top sheet pulled back over
      the edge of the bed.
It hasn't dissolved back into nothing, into reality.
Through the open window, sea air, smelling of iodine.

Early morning: a man calling a small boy back from the water.
That small boy— he would be twenty now.

派斯克島

每個生命都有那麼一兩分鐘
都有那麼一個房間，在海邊或山裡

桌上一盤杏子，杏核在白菸灰缸

一如所有印象，這些是整體狀況：
陽光顫動在你臉頰
我的手指壓住你的唇
藍白牆壁，矮櫃子稍稍落了漆

那房間一定還在，在四樓
面海有個小陽台
正方形白房間，床罩拉到床沿
一切還沒褪入空無，褪入現實
敞開的窗飄進海風，碘的味道

大清早，一名男子呼喊一個小男孩上岸
小男孩現在該有二十歲了

Around your face, rushes of damp hair, streaked with
   auburn.
Muslin, flicker of silver. Heavy jar filled with white peonies.

你臉上幾綹亂髮，濕答答，參差著赭紅
棉麻褐，銀光閃爍。沉甸甸一整甕白牡丹

Retreating Light

You were like very young children,
always waiting for a story.
And I'd been through it all too many times;
I was tired of telling stories.
So I gave you the pencil and paper.
I gave you pens made of reeds
I had gathered myself, afternoons in the dense meadows.
I told you, write your own story.

After all those years of listening
I thought you'd know
what a story was.

All you could do was weep.
You wanted everything told to you
and nothing thought through yourselves.

Then I realized you couldn't think
with any real boldness or passion;
you hadn't had your own lives yet,

退隱的光

你們就像小小孩

總是等著聽故事

而故事我說了一遍又一遍

已經全說膩了

所以我給你們鉛筆和紙，給你們

我下午在茂盛的草原

親手採集的蘆葦

做成的筆，要你們自己寫故事

聽了這麼多年故事

我以為你們已經知道

甚麼是故事

但你們只會哭

只想聽命行事

完全不想自己動腦筋

我也發現你們沒法

真正熱情大膽地思考

你們還沒有自己的生命

your own tragedies.
So I gave you lives, I gave you tragedies,
because apparently tools alone weren't enough.

You will never know how deeply
it pleases me to see you sitting there
like independent beings,
to see you dreaming by the open window,
holding the pencils I gave you
until the summer morning disappears into writing.

Creation has brought you
great excitement, as I knew it would,
as it does in the beginning.
And I am free to do as I please now,
to attend to other things, in confidence
you have no need of me anymore.

還沒有自己的悲劇

所以我給你們生命，給你們悲劇

因為，顯然，只有工具並不夠

你們永遠不知道我多麼

多麼欣慰看你們坐在那兒

像個獨立個體

看你們在敞開的窗邊

做夢，握著我給你們的筆

直到夏日清晨化入文字

如我預期，創作

帶給你們的強烈喜悅

一如鴻濛初啟

於是現在我能自由自在

去照應別的事；有了自信

你們不再需要我

Vespers

I know what you planned, what you meant to do, teaching me
to love the world, making it impossible
to turn away completely, to shut it out completely
    ever again—
it is everywhere; when I close my eyes,
birdsong, scent of lilac in early spring, scent of summer roses:
you mean to take it away, each flower, each connection
    with earth—
why would you wound me, why would you want me
desolate in the end, unless you wanted me so starved for hope
I would refuse to see that finally
nothing was left to me, and would believe instead
in the end you were left to me.

晚禱

我知道祢的計謀，知道祢有意

教導我愛這世界，讓我無法全然

掉頭而去，全然避開它——

它無所不在，當我閉起眼

鳥聲，早春丁香的芬芳，夏日玫瑰的芬芳

而祢有意把它全奪走，這每一朵花，每一種與大地的聯繫——

祢為甚麼要傷害我，為甚麼要我

荒蕪以終，除非祢想讓我極度饑渴於

希望，以致拒絕看清

自己終究一無所有，轉而相信終究

我還有祢

Vespers: Parousia

Love of my life, you
are lost and I am
young again.

A few years pass.
The air fills
with girlish music;
in the front yard
the apple tree is
studded with blossoms.

I try to win you back,
that is the point
of the writing.
But you are gone forever,
as in Russian novels, saying
a few words I don't remember—

How lush the world is,
how full of things that don't belong to me—

晚禱：復臨

我生命之愛，祢
失蹤了而我
又回復了青春

多年過去了
空氣裡充滿
女孩兒調調的音樂
前院
蘋果樹
點綴著花

我試著重新贏得祢
這是我
寫作的原因
但祢永遠離開了
像在俄國小說裡，說一些
我記不得的話——

世界如此豐滿
如此充滿不屬於我的東西——

I watch the blossoms shatter,
no longer pink,
but old, old, a yellowish white—
the petals seem
to float on the bright grass,
fluttering slightly.

What a nothing you were,
to be changed so quickly
into an image, an odor—
you are everywhere, source
of wisdom and anguish.

我看著花朵散落

不再粉紅

老了，老了，發黃的白──

花瓣彷彿漂浮

在鮮亮草地

輕輕顫動

曾經祢甚麼都不是

迅速被轉化

變成一個形象，一種氣味──

現在祢無所不在，祢是

智慧和痛苦之源

Vespers

Your voice is gone now; I hardly hear you.
Your starry voice all shadow now
and the earth dark again
with your great changes of heart.

And by day the grass going brown in places
under the broad shadows of the maple trees.
Now, everywhere I am talked to by silence

so it is clear I have no access to you;
I do not exist for you, you have drawn
a line through my name.

In what contempt do you hold us
to believe only loss can impress
your power on us,

the first rains of autumn shaking the white lilies—

晚禱

祢的聲音消失了，我幾乎聽不見祢
祢星光般的聲音現在全是陰影
隨著祢變化巨大的
心，大地又回歸幽暗

到了白天，寬闊的楓樹蔭下
草地漸漸枯黃
現在四周只有沉默對我說話

所以情況很明白：我無從接近祢
對祢，我並不存在，祢已經槓掉了
我的名字

祢是怎樣輕視我們
以為只有失去
能讓我們感受祢的力量

好比第一場秋雨撼動白百合——

When you go, you go absolutely,
deducting visible life from all things

but not all life,
lest we turn from you.

當祢離開，祢離開得斷然

決然，帶走所有可見的生命

而不是所有生命

免得我們棄祢而去

Vespers

End of August. Heat
like a tent over
John's garden. And some things
have the nerve to be getting started,
clusters of tomatoes, stands
of late lilies— optimism
of the great stalks— imperial
gold and silver: but why
start anything
so close to the end?
Tomatoes that will never ripen, lilies
winter will kill, that won't
come back in spring. Or
are you thinking
I spend too much time
looking ahead, like
an old woman wearing
sweaters in summer;
are you saying I can
flourish, having

晚禱

八月末。暑氣

像一頂帳篷

籠罩約翰的花園,而有些東西

竟有膽量開始生長

成串成串番茄,一枝枝

晚開的百合——這是

優秀品種的樂觀,高貴的

金色銀色。但為甚麼

要在這麼接近結束的時候

才開始?永遠

不會熟的番茄,終究要被寒冬

斫殺,到了春天

不會再出現的百合。或者

祢是不是以為

我浪費太多時間

瞻前顧後

像個老太婆,在夏天

還不肯脫毛衣

祢是不是說我也能

枝繁葉茂就算

no hope

of enduring? Blaze of the red cheek, glory

of the open throat, white,

spotted with crimson.

沒希望

持續長久？這臉頰酡紅的光彩

喉嚨敞開的榮耀

血色斑斑的　白

Sunset

My great happiness
is the sound your voice makes
calling to me even in despair; my sorrow
that I cannot answer you
in speech you accept as mine.

You have no faith in your own language.
So you invest
authority in signs
you cannot read with any accuracy.

And yet your voice reaches me always.
And I answer constantly,
my anger passing
as winter passes. My tenderness
should be apparent to you
in the breeze of summer evening
and in the words that become
your own response.

日落

我強烈的快樂來自

聽到你呼喚我的聲音

就算在絕望中；我的悲哀是

我無法回覆你

以你認定我該有的口吻

你對自己的言語沒有信心

所以你把權威

託付給你完全無法

正確解讀的符碼

但你的聲音仍然

傳達給了我

我也不斷回覆你

我的怒氣像寒冬過境

過去了，我的溫柔

對你應該很明顯，它展現

在夏夜的微風，在你

自我應答的文字

Lullaby

Time to rest now; you have had
enough excitement for the time being.

Twilight, then early evening. Fireflies
in the room, flickering here and there, here and there,
and summer's deep sweetness filling the open window.

Don't think of these things any more.
Listen to my breathing, your own breathing
like the fireflies, each small breath
a flare in which the world appears.

I've sung to you long enough in the summer night.
I'll win you over in the end; the world can't give you
this sustained vision.

You must be taught to love me. Human beings must be
        taught to love
silence and darkness.

安眠曲

休息時間到了。這時
你該興奮夠了

薄暮，之後入夜。螢火蟲
在屋裡閃爍，這裡那裡那裡這裡
夏季的濃濃甜味填滿了敞開的窗

別再想這些事了。聽聽
我的呼吸，你自己的呼吸
像螢火蟲，每一微弱呼吸
是一抹微光，世界就呈現其中

我已經在夏夜對你唱得夠久了
終究我會贏得你；這世界無法給你同樣
持久的關注

你得學會愛我。人得學會愛上
沉默，和黑暗

The Silver Lily

The nights have grown cool again, like the nights
of early spring, and quiet again. Will
speech disturb you? We're
alone now; we have no reason for silence.

Can you see, over the garden—the full moon rises.
I won't see the next full moon.

In spring, when the moon rose, it meant
time was endless. Snowdrops
opened and closed, the clustered
seeds of the maples fell in pale drifts.
White over white, the moon rose over the birch tree.
And in the crook, where the tree divides,
leaves of the first daffodils, in moonlight
soft greenish-silver.

We have come too far together toward the end now
to fear the end. These nights, I am no longer even certain
I know what the end means. And you, who've been
          with a man—

銀色百合

夜晚又變涼了
像早春夜晚，而且又安靜了——
說話會干擾你嗎？現在
四下無人，我們沒理由保持沉默

你看見了嗎，花園上方——滿月升起
下一個滿月我就看不到了

在春天，月亮升起
表示時間一無止盡。雪花蓮
開了謝了，楓樹種子
一群群無力飄落
月亮升起越過白樺，白色重疊白色
拐角裡，樹的分界處
最先竄出的水仙嫩葉在月光下
發出柔軟的銀綠

迢遙長路我們並肩前往終點，現在
再不怕終點了。這些夜晚我甚至懷疑我是否
了解終點的意義。而你，有男人為伴的你——

after the first cries,

doesn't joy, like fear, make no sound?

最初的驚叫之後，喜悅

不就像恐懼，同樣無聲？

September Twilight

I gathered you together,
I can dispense with you—

I'm tired of you, chaos
of the living world—
I can only extend myself
for so long to a living thing.

I summoned you into existence
by opening my mouth, by lifting
my little finger, shimmering

blues of the wild
aster, blossom
of the lily, immense,
gold-veined—

you come and go; eventually
I forget your names.

九月薄暮

我把你們聚在一起
我可以不要你們

我對你們厭倦了，這
生物世界的混亂——
對一種生物，我能付出的
時間有限

我開個口，舉一根
我的小指頭，你們就應召
現形，亮閃閃

藍色的野生
紫菀花，盛開的
百合，碩大
金色紋理——

你們來來去去，終於
我忘了你們的名字

You come and go, every one of you
flawed in some way,
in some way compromised: you are worth
one life, no more than that.

I gathered you together;
I can erase you
as though you were a draft to be thrown away,
an exercise

because I've finished you, vision
of deepest mourning.

你們來來去去，一無例外
各有瑕疵
各有妥協：你們只配
活一次，最多一次

我把你們聚在一起
可以把你們擦掉
當你們是要丟棄的草稿
一件習作

因為我已經了結了你們──
最深沉哀傷的幻象

The Gold Lily

As I perceive
I am dying now and know
I will not speak again, will not
survive the earth, be summoned
out of it again, not
a flower yet, a spine only, raw dirt
catching my ribs, I call you,
father and master: all around,
my companions are failing, thinking
you do not see. How
can they know you see
unless you save us?
In the summer twilight, are you
close enough to hear
your child's terror? Or
are you not my father,
you who raised me?

金色百合

當我意識到

我正瀕臨死亡，知道

自己再也無法開口，不能

倖免於大地，也不會

被再度召喚，還不成其花朵

只是一根脊柱，粗糙的土

絆住我肋骨，我呼喚祢

我父，我主：四面八方

我的同伴全都敗下陣來，以為

祢視若無睹。他們如何知道

祢看到了，除非

祢出手搭救？

在這夏日薄暮，祢

靠得夠近聽得見祢孩子的

恐懼嗎？或者

養育我的

祢，其實並非我父？

The White Lilies

As a man and woman make
a garden between them like
a bed of stars, here
they linger in the summer evening
and the evening turns
cold with their terror: it
could all end, it is capable
of devastation. All, all
can be lost, through scented air
the narrow columns
uselessly rising, and beyond,
a churning sea of poppies—

Hush, beloved. It doesn't matter to me
how many summers I live to return:
this one summer we have entered eternity.
I felt your two hands
bury me to release its splendor.

白百合

一男一女
把兩人之間的花園整理得
像一床繁星，他們流連
在花園的夏夜
而夜在他們的恐懼中
轉涼：一切
可能全部結束，崩毀是
可能的。一切，一切
都可能消失，穿越芬芳的
空氣，纖細的莖一根根
無謂地抽高，稍遠
罌粟花翻騰如海——

別出聲，親愛的。我並不在乎
我能重來多少個夏季
就憑這一個夏季我們已經進入永恆
我感覺你以雙手
埋葬了我，釋放出其中光彩

國家圖書館預行編目資料

野鳶尾／露伊絲・葛綠珂(Louise Glück)
著. 陳育虹譯. --初版. --臺北市:寶瓶文
化, 2017. 2
面; 公分. --(Island;264)
譯自:*The Wild Iris*
ISBN 978-986-406-077-1 (平裝)

874.51   106000479

Island 264

野鳶尾

作者／露伊絲・葛綠珂(Louise Glück)　　　譯者／陳育虹

發行人／張寶琴
社長兼總編輯／朱亞君
副總編輯／張純玲
資深編輯／丁慧瑋　編輯／林婕伃
美術主編／林慧雯
校對／賴逸娟・陳佩伶・劉素芬・陳育虹
營銷部主任／林歆婕　業務專員／林裕翔　企劃專員／李祉萱
財務／莊玉萍
出版者／寶瓶文化事業股份有限公司
地址／台北市110信義區基隆路一段180號8樓
電話／(02) 27494988　傳真／(02) 27495072
郵政劃撥／19446403　寶瓶文化事業股份有限公司
印刷廠／世和印製企業有限公司
總經銷／大和書報圖書股份有限公司　電話／(02) 89902588
地址／新北市新莊區五工五路2號　傳真／(02) 22997900
E-mail／aquarius@udngroup.com
版權所有・翻印必究
法律顧問／理律法律事務所陳長文律師、蔣大中律師
如有破損或裝訂錯誤,請寄回本公司更換
著作完成日期／一九九二年
初版一刷日期／二〇一七年二月七日
初版七刷+日期／二〇二三年十一月三日
ISBN／978-986-406-077-1
定價／二八〇元

AQUARIUS

寶瓶
文化事業

愛書人卡

感謝您熱心的為我們填寫，
對您的意見，我們會認真的加以參考，
希望寶瓶文化推出的每一本書，都能得到您的肯定與永遠的支持。

系列：Island 264　　**書名：野鳶尾**

1. 姓名：_____　性別：□男　□女

2. 生日：_____年_____月_____日

3. 教育程度：□大學以上　□大學　□專科　□高中、高職　□高中職以下

4. 職業：_____

5. 聯絡地址：_____

　　聯絡電話：_____　　手機：_____

6. E-mail信箱：_____

　　　　　　□同意　□不同意　免費獲得寶瓶文化叢書訊息

7. 購買日期：_____ 年 _____ 月 _____日

8. 您得知本書的管道：□報紙／雜誌　□電視／電台　□親友介紹　□逛書店　□網路
　　□傳單／海報　□廣告　□其他

9. 您在哪裡買到本書：□書店，店名_____　□劃撥　□現場活動　□贈書
　　□網路購書，網站名稱：_____　□其他_____

10. 對本書的建議：（請填代號　1. 滿意　2. 尚可　3. 再改進，請提供意見）

　　內容：_____

　　封面：_____

　　編排：_____

　　其他：_____

　　綜合意見：_____

11. 希望我們未來出版哪一類的書籍：_____

讓文字與書寫的聲音大鳴大放
寶瓶文化事業股份有限公司

（請沿此虛線剪下）